Pouch!

David Ezra Stein

G. P. Putnam's Sons   Penguin Young Readers Group

For Nile

G. P. PUTNAM'S SONS

A division of Penguin Young Readers Group.

Published by The Penguin Group.

Penguin Group (USA) Inc., 375 Hudson Street, New York, NY 10014, U.S.A.

Penguin Group (Canada), 90 Eglinton Avenue East, Suite 700, Toronto, Ontario M4P 2Y3, Canada (a division of Pearson Penguin Canada Inc.).

Penguin Books Ltd, 80 Strand, London WC2R 0RL, England.

Penguin Ireland, 25 St. Stephen's Green, Dublin 2, Ireland (a division of Penguin Books Ltd.).

Penguin Group (Australia), 250 Camberwell Road, Camberwell, Victoria 3124, Australia (a division of Pearson Australia Group Pty Ltd).

Penguin Books India Pvt Ltd, 11 Community Centre, Panchsheel Park, New Delhi - 110 017, India.

Penguin Group (NZ), 67 Apollo Drive, Rosedale, North Shore 0632, New Zealand (a division of Pearson New Zealand Ltd).

Penguin Books (South Africa) (Pty) Ltd, 24 Sturdee Avenue, Rosebank, Johannesburg 2196, South Africa.

Penguin Books Ltd, Registered Offices: 80 Strand, London WC2R 0RL, England.

Manufactured in China by South China Printing Co. Ltd. Design by Katrina Damkoehler. Text set in Woodland ITC Medium. The art was created with china marker, watercolors, and water-soluble crayon.

Library of Congress Cataloging-in-Publication Data

Stein, David Ezra.

Pouch! / David Ezra Stein.   p. cm.

Summary: A baby kangaroo takes his first tentative hops outside of his mama's pouch, meeting other creatures and growing bolder each time.

[1. Growth—Fiction. 2. Self-confidence—Fiction. 3. Kangaroos—Fiction. 4. Animals—Infancy—Fiction. 5. Mother and child—Fiction.] I. Title.

PZ7.S8179Po 2009   [E]—dc22   2008053558

ISBN 978-0-399-25051-4

Special Markets ISBN 978-0-399-25512-0

Not for resale

3 5 7 9 10 8 6 4 2

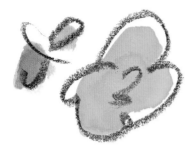

When he was a brand-new kangaroo,

Joey lived in the pouch. Until one day . . .

. . . he peeked out and saw the world,

and his mama smiling down at him.

He climbed
out of the
pouch and
took two hops to the tall grass.

Pouch!

said Joey.

But soon he
wanted to hop again.

He took

three hops

to the little hill.

POUCH!

said

Joey.

But soon he
wanted to hop again.

He took
four hops
to the sandy hollow.

said
Joey.

But soon he wanted to hop again.

He took five hops
to the pasture fence.

Kangaroo.

said the two kangaroos.

"Wait!" said Joey. "You were afraid of me, too?"

Then they hop,

hop, hop, hop,

hoppity-hopped

everywhere!

Pouch?

said the mamas.

No, thanks.